A Piece of Cake

TO DEAR PAT TUPPER AND ALL THE FAMILY

WITH TONS OF LOVE AS EVER

First published 1989 by Walker Books Ltd
87 Vauxhall Walk, London SE11 5HJ

© 1989 Jill Murphy

This edition published 1991

4 6 8 10 9 7 5

Printed in Hong Kong

British Library Cataloguing in Publication Data
A catalogue record for this book is
available from the British Library.
ISBN 0-7445-2016-9

A Piece of Cake

Jill Murphy

WALKER BOOKS

AND SUBSIDIARIES

LONDON • BOSTON • SYDNEY

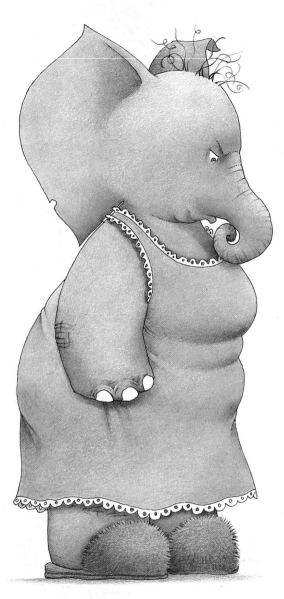

"I'm fat," said Mrs Large.

"No you're not," said Lester.

"You're our cuddly mummy," said Laura.

"You're *just* right," said Luke.

"Mummy's got wobbly bits," said the baby.

"Exactly," said Mrs Large. "As I was saying – I'm fat."

"We must all go on a diet," said Mrs Large.
"No more cakes. No more biscuits. No more
crisps. No more sitting around all day.
From now on, it's healthy living."

"Can we watch TV?" asked Lester, as they
trooped in from school.
"Certainly not!" said Mrs Large. "We're all
off for a nice healthy jog round the park."
And they were.

"What's for tea, Mum?" asked Laura
when they arrived home.
"Some nice healthy watercress soup," said
Mrs Large. "Followed by a nice healthy cup
of water."
"Oh!" said Laura. "That sounds . . . nice."

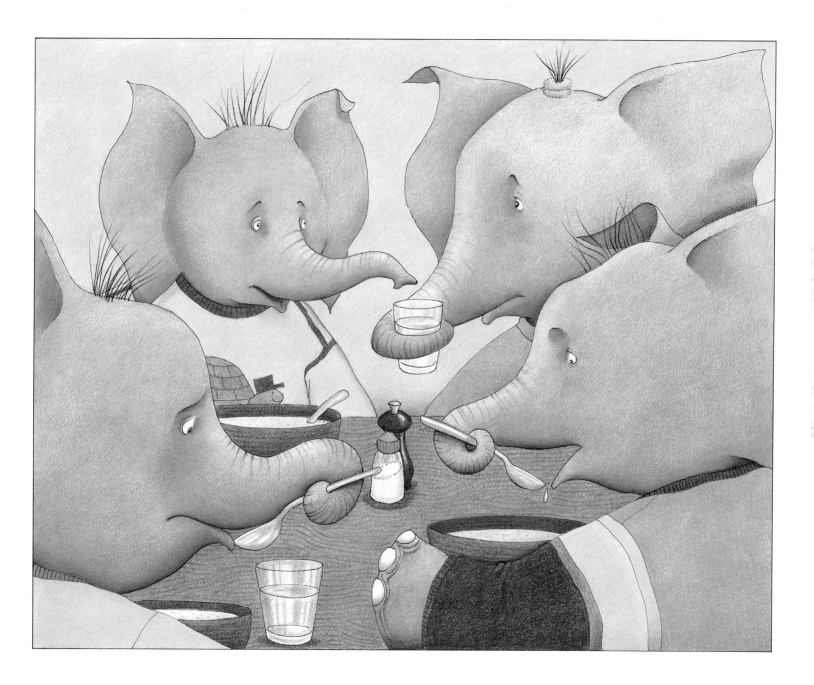

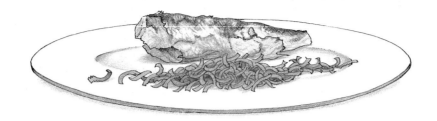

"I'm just going to watch the news, dear,"
   said Mr Large when he came home from work.
"No you're not, dear," said Mrs Large.
"You're off for a nice healthy jog round
   the park, followed by your tea – a delicious
   sardine with grated carrot."
"I can't wait," said Mr Large.

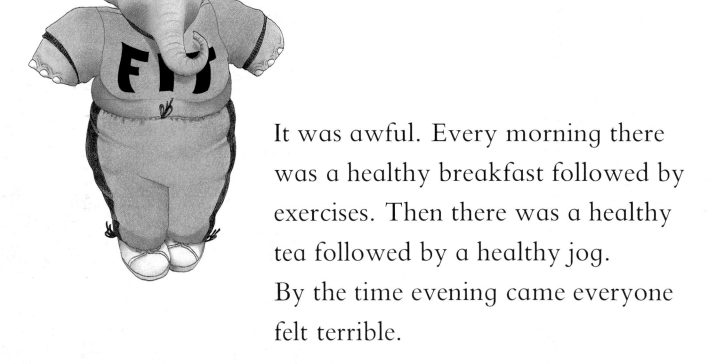

It was awful. Every morning there was a healthy breakfast followed by exercises. Then there was a healthy tea followed by a healthy jog.
By the time evening came everyone felt terrible.

"We aren't getting any thinner, dear,"
said Mr Large.

"Perhaps elephants are *meant* to be fat,"
said Luke.

"Nonsense!" said Mrs Large. "We mustn't
give up now."

"Wibbly-wobbly, wibbly-wobbly," went
the baby.

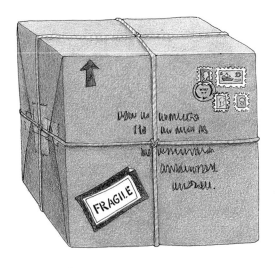

One morning a parcel arrived. It was a cake
from Granny. Everyone stared at it hopefully.
Mrs Large put it into the cupboard on a high
shelf. "Just in case we have visitors,"she
said sternly.

Everyone kept thinking about the cake.
They thought about it during tea. They
thought about it during the healthy jog.
They thought about it in bed that night.
Mrs Large sat up. "I can't stand it any
more," she said to herself. "I must have
a piece of that cake."

Mrs Large crept out of bed and went
downstairs to the kitchen. She took a knife
out of the drawer and opened the cupboard.
There was only one piece of cake left!

"Ah ha!" said Mr Large, seeing the knife.
"Caught in the act!"
  Mrs Large switched on the light and saw
  Mr Large and all the children hiding
  under the table.
"There *is* one piece left," said Laura in
  a helpful way.

Mrs Large began to laugh. "We're all as
bad as each other!" she said, eating the
last piece of cake before anyone else did.
"I do think elephants are meant to be fat,"
said Luke.
"I think you're probably right, dear," said
Mrs Large.
"Wibbly-wobbly, wibbly-wobbly!" went
the baby.

MORE WALKER PAPERBACKS
For You to Enjoy

Also by Jill Murphy

FIVE MINUTES' PEACE

Winner of the Best Book for Babies Award

All Mrs Large wants is a few minutes' peace in the bath away from the children.
But the little Larges have other ideas!

0-7445-0918-1   £4.50

ALL IN ONE PIECE

Highly Commended for the Kate Greenaway Medal

Shortlisted for the Children's Book Award

While Mr and Mrs Large get ready to go out for the evening,
Laura, Lester, Luke and the baby are busy making a mess!

0-7445-0933-5   £4.50

GEOFFREY STRANGEWAYS

Geoffrey Strangeways is a boy with a burning ambition: to be a knight!

"Jill Murphy can only add to her reputation with this hilarious tale… A book
to keep children laughing up to around the age of ten."

The School Librarian

0-7445-1722-2   £2.99

Walker Paperbacks are available from most booksellers, or by post from B.B.C.S., P.O. Box 941, Hull, North Humberside HU1 3YQ

24 hour telephone credit card line 01482 224626

To order, send: Title, author, ISBN number and price for each book ordered, your full name and address,
cheque or postal order payable to BBCS for the total amount and allow the following for postage and packing:
UK and BFPO: £1.00 for the first book, and 50p for each additional book to a maximum of £3.50.
Overseas and Eire: £2.00 for the first book, £1.00 for the second and 50p for each additional book.

Prices and availability are subject to change without notice.